Waltham Forest Libraries

Please return this item by the last date stamped. The loan may be renewed unless required by another customer.

09120		

Need to renew your books?
http://www.walthamforest.gov.uk/libraries or
Dial 0333 370 4700 for Callpoint – our 24/7 automated telephone renewal line. You will need your library card number and your PIN. If you do not know your PIN, contact your local library.

For Mum, with love

– Lara

For Jules, who makes me smile like Mo

– Becky

Midge
& Mo

STRIPES PUBLISHING LTD
An imprint of the Little Tiger Group
1 Coda Studios,
189 Munster Road,
London SW6 6AW

First published in Great Britain in 2020

Text copyright © Lara Williamson, 2020
Illustrations copyright © Becky Cameron, 2020

ISBN: 978-1-78895-111-1

Printed and bound in China.

STP/1800/0266/0419

2 4 6 8 10 9 7 5 3 1

Midge & Mo

Lara Williamson & Becky Cameron

stripes

Midge is small.

The school is big.

Mr Lupin, the teacher, is very big.

"Welcome to our school, Midge,"
he says.

Mr Lupin smiles
and his smile
is big, too.

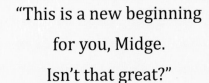

"This is a new beginning
for you, Midge.
Isn't that great?"

Midge does not think it's great.
He doesn't want a new
beginning or a new school
or a very smiley teacher.

And even though his
mum tried to explain to
him that new beginnings
and looking forwards could
be good things, Midge
doesn't think they are.

Instead, he
wants things to
go back to the
way they were.

"Let's give Midge a welcome clap," says Mr Lupin. "We hope you enjoy our school."

Everyone claps and Midge stares out at all the friendly, happy faces, and then looks down at his shoes.

He thinks: *how can I enjoy it when I want everything to go backwards?*

Midge tells himself: *if I was on a bike, I'd make it go backwards not forwards. If I could, I'd walk backwards, too. I don't want to look forwards, even if Mum says so.*

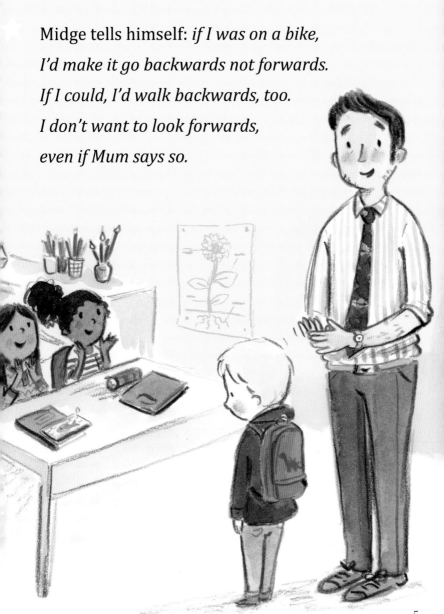

Mr Lupin points to a girl at
the back of the class.

"Mo, can you come here please?"

The girl's face breaks into a huge
smile and she races up to the front.

She grins at Midge and then whispers
"hello", but Midge doesn't say hello back.

Mr Lupin explains that Mo is going
to be Midge's buddy.

"Mo will show you around school
and look after you. When you're new
you need a friendly face."

Midge thinks Mo definitely
has a friendly face.

"It'll be fun," whispers Mo, and
she gives Midge another big smile. "I know
all the best places to play. We can be
friends, can't we?"

Midge doesn't answer and although Mo is a little bit disappointed she doesn't stop smiling. Midge wishes there was no such thing as new beginnings. He wishes he could climb into a rocket and lift off. Then he'd fly away from this new school back to his old school.

Only I can't, because everything has changed, thinks Midge.

Mr Lupin pipes up, "Can you show Midge where to put his coat, Mo?" He gives Midge an encouraging smile. "Then you can take a seat in the empty chair next to Mo."

9

Mo takes Midge to the cloakroom to hang up his coat, then races back into the classroom. "It's the best seat in the class because it's near Rex's cage. He's the class hamster," Mo explains, hooking her arm through Midge's and leading him over to the cage.

"Rex is very friendly. Do you have any pets?
I have a dog called Noodle."

Rex

Midge shakes his head and sits
down in the empty seat. Mo thinks that this
isn't how she imagined being a buddy but
she smiles anyway. Midge doesn't smile back.
Instead he feels sad, like there's an invisible
rain cloud hanging over his head.
Drip-drip-drip.

He thinks about how
Mum and Dad have separated,
and he remembers how they
used to build sandcastles
together and go kite flying.

Suddenly, Midge's eyes feel prickly.

At lunchtime, the gloomy rain cloud follows Midge.

It's there when he eats lunch.

Drip-drip-drip.

Mum's made his favourite sandwiches. She's put a note with a smiley face inside his lunchbox saying:

I love you,
mum ×
☺

Midge doesn't have a
smiley face though, even
when Mo sits down beside
him and says, "You can have
one of my biscuits."

Midge shakes his head.
He doesn't want a biscuit.

15

After lunch, the rain cloud is still there when
Mo shows Midge the playground. She says,
"This is where we play football." Mo grabs a ball
and kicks it. A boy waves and kicks it straight back.
Midge thinks of how he used to play football
and score goals at his old school.

Midge misses football but most of all,
Midge misses his old friends. Mo smiles and
picks up the ball. "Would you like to play?"

Midge shakes his head. Why should he play
football when he feels this sad? The rain
cloud would only follow him and make him feel
like it was raining on his head all the time.
Drip-drip-drip.

"It'll be lots of fun," says Mo, grinning.

Midge can't help noticing how much Mo smiles.
Her smile is twice as big as Mr Lupin's.

She smiled at Midge
when he first walked
into the classroom.

She smiled when
she showed him
the book corner.

Mo even smiled when she fetched a piece of paper and made Midge a label for his coat hook. She wrote his name in big swirly letters, then she drew a sun and coloured it in and she smiled again as she stuck it above Midge's coat.

Mo smiled A LOT.

Even now, Mo is smiling when she says, "If you don't want to play football, that's OK."

Next, Mo takes Midge to a little flower patch at the top end of the playground.

"This is our special flower garden," says Mo, pointing towards it. "We plant seeds here and watch them grow."

Midge stares at the garden and the small
painted sign in the earth saying:

FRIENDSHIP IS LIKE
A PLANT—WHEN YOU
TAKE CARE OF IT,
IT GROWS.

Midge isn't sure what it means but
it's a nice sign all the same.

Mo's eyes widen. "Look," she says,
grabbing Midge by the arm.

"That sunflower is growing so tall. We moved it from another spot because it's sunnier near the wall. We didn't think it would like the change but we looked after it and now it's really tall. I bet we see the petals soon."

Mo smiles her brightest smile.

Midge doesn't care whether the
sunflower is growing.

He doesn't care about the flower patch.

He doesn't want to talk.

"Come on," says Mo.
"There's lots more to show you.
Let me take you to the Trim Trail.
It's the best."

At the Trim Trail, Midge doesn't hang off
the bars even though Mo does.

Swinging like a monkey,
she goes from bar to bar, whooping with
happiness. "Have a try," urges Mo.

Dropping down, Mo runs over to a low wooden
pole and pretends she's walking the tightrope.

"Imagine me in a circus," yells Mo.
"I'm high up in the big top. The audience
are 'oohing' and 'ahhing.'"

Next there's one wobble … two … three…
Mo slips off the pole and then, grinning, runs to
the tyre swing and pushes her body through it.

"Look, now I'm like a mole peeping through a hole."

28

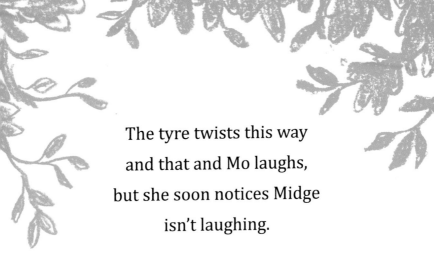

The tyre twists this way
and that and Mo laughs,
but she soon notices Midge
isn't laughing.

Mo stops.

"Would you like to play on
anything, Midge?"

Midge shakes his head
firmly and walks over to the
big tree and sits down.

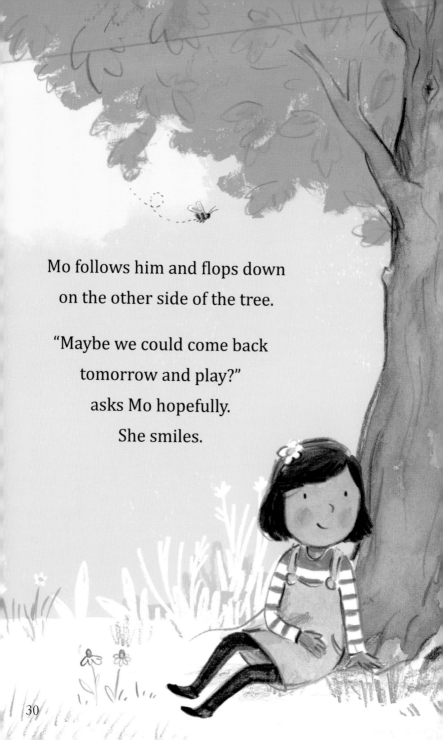

Mo follows him and flops down
on the other side of the tree.

"Maybe we could come back
tomorrow and play?"
asks Mo hopefully.
She smiles.

Midge doesn't answer and
he definitely doesn't smile.

Lunchtime is over and Midge still hasn't said a word. He didn't even laugh when they were walking back to class and Mo showed him her best funny faces.

Everyone else laughed though.

"Hey, Mo, do some more faces,"
everyone shouted.

And she did.

They laughed even harder when Mo said,
"What do elves learn at school?
The elf-a-bet."

Midge didn't laugh.
He looked as sad as a clown
whose smile was upside down.

"I hope you've all had a lovely lunch break," says Mr Lupin as everyone sits down in the classroom.

"We're going to do some art this afternoon. I'd like you to draw a picture of your day. All the colouring pencils are at the back of the class, go and help yourself."

Mo picks a *rainbow* of colours.

Midge picks grey.

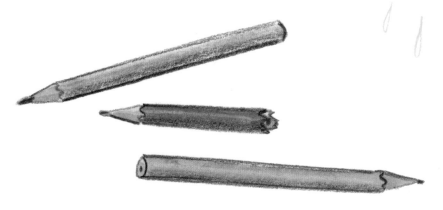

"Would you like to use some of my colours?"
asks Mo.

She pushes the pot of colouring pencils
towards Midge and smiles, but Midge
pushes it back, shaking his head.

Midge draws grey raindrops.

Mo draws with a rainbow of colours.

When she's finished she shows her picture to Midge and says, "It's us looking at the flower patch." Midge stares at it. There is a big sun, lots of green plants and butterflies. Everything is big and bright. Underneath Mo has written 'Midge and Mo'. In the picture Mo has a big smile and Midge doesn't.

Midge looks down at the raindrops he's scribbled on his paper.
Drip-drip-drip.

When Mr Lupin collects the drawings he says, "They're great. I'm going to put them on the wall next to each other. It's lovely to see sunshine and rain together."

The next day, as soon as Mo reaches
the school playground, she heads
straight for Midge.

Mo zips around Midge in a circle.

"Wheeee!"

"It's my new scooter," says Mo.
"Would you like a go, Midge?"

Midge shakes his head.

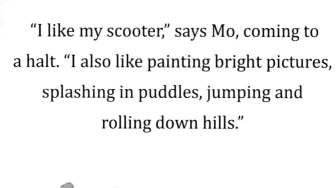

"I like my scooter," says Mo, coming to a halt. "I also like painting bright pictures, splashing in puddles, jumping and rolling down hills."

"What do *you* like,
Midge?" asks Mo, parking
her scooter carefully.

Midge thinks for
a second.

He liked everything
the way it was before
but he doesn't
say so.

"Another thing I like is having
fun with my friends," adds Mo.

Midge thinks for a second, remembering
his friends at his old school. They loved
puddles and jumping and rolling down hills
and painting bright pictures, too.

Midge misses having fun.

Mo gives Midge her best smile.
"You can have so much fun with
a friend," she says.

Next, Mo shrugs off her
backpack and grabs a ball.
"Come and play football with me,
Midge. I know you didn't want to
yesterday but let's play now."
She runs across the playground.

Midge doesn't move.
"You can shoot all the goals
if you want." Mo smiles and
waves at Midge, but Midge
doesn't wave back so Mo
kicks the ball towards him.

It rolls across the playground
and stops at Midge's feet,
but he just stares at it.

Then he walks away and sits down under the big tree again. Midge stares as Mo fetches the ball and he watches as she asks the other children if they want to play.

Everyone comes running and they squeal, "Yes. Let's play, Mo." Every so often Mo turns to look at Midge and she smiles, but Midge pretends to look at his shoes.

When it starts to rain,
Mo puts the ball away
and appears with a
bright umbrella.

"Come and share
my umbrella, Midge.
There's enough space
for two."

But Midge shakes his head.
He doesn't want an umbrella.

In Art, Mo watches as Midge stares out
at the rain, then silently draws a train that
will take him to the moon.

In English, Mo watches Midge as he gazes
at the ceiling, then writes a story about a dragon
who can't breathe fire any more.

In Geography, Mr Lupin asks
everyone what they think of
volcanoes.

But Midge doesn't join in.
He doesn't say one word all morning.

At lunchtime, Midge leaves the
classroom without Mo. "Is everything
OK, Mo?" asks Mr Lupin.

Mo shakes her head. "I'm trying to be
a buddy to Midge … but he doesn't speak."

"It might be because Midge is new and
everything is strange to him," said Mr Lupin.

Mo stares at her shoes, like Midge does.
"But Midge doesn't want to be *my* friend.
I've tried everything," she whispers.

"Don't give up, Mo," says Mr Lupin.
"Nothing is in the right place for Midge
at the moment. Perhaps he doesn't feel
like he's in the right place either.
New beginnings can feel like that."

Mo nods.

"You were new here once," continues Mr Lupin.

"That's why I asked you to be Midge's buddy, because I was sure you would remember how your first day here felt, too."

Mo thinks back and she can remember.

It was last year and if she thinks really hard Mo can remember not wanting to eat her lunch on her first day, even though Mum had written a little note saying:

I love you – Mum x

She remembers how she watched the other children playing football but didn't join in. Instead, she sat under the same tree as Midge.

She remembers
feeling sad.

She remembers a gift that her mum and dad
gave her to help her feel better.

Mo smiles and looks up at Mr Lupin.
"I'm going to keep trying with Midge.
Because that's what friends are for."

Mr Lupin smiles right back.

After school, Mo rushes home and heads straight up to her room. She reaches up to her shelf.

The little globe with a boat inside is there in its usual spot between her books and her piggy bank. It was the gift given to Mo by her mum and dad when she started at her new school and they told her to shake it whenever she felt sad.

Mo felt sad a lot back then. She took it everywhere she went.

"Look," said Dad. "It's like
rain is falling on your little ship."

"It looks like teardrops to me,"
Mo whispered.

"You're right," said
Mum. "Raindrops
and teardrops. Both
are important."

"How are
teardrops
important?"
asked Mo.

"We need rain in our lives because it helps things grow," Dad explained. "Tears can help, too, because no one BIG or small can go through life without feeling sad sometimes."

Then Mum added, "It's OK to feel sad and even if it lasts for a while it won't last for ever."

Mo nodded. "After it rains, what happens next?"

"The sun comes out,"
Dad smiled. "After the rain we have sun
and after tears things can get brighter, too."

"Now when you feel sad you can shake the globe and the little boat will carry away the teardrops and remind you that the sun is coming. Maybe not today, maybe not tomorrow, but one day soon."

"That's right," agreed Mum, hugging Mo. "You'll feel better soon."

Mo shook the globe a lot in the beginning because she felt sad about all the changes and being the new girl. But as the days passed, Mo made new friends and she felt brighter, so she didn't shake the globe so much.

After tea, Mo explains to Mum and Dad
what she wants to do.

Mum helps by finding the perfect empty jar.
She fills it with water and a tiny bit of
baby oil and some glitter.

Noodle doesn't help but he does wag his tail.

Dad helps by sticking a tiny boat that Mo
found in her toybox on the inside of the lid.
Then he screws the lid back on the jar...

...and turns everything upside down.

The glitter falls.

Mo watches it.

Dad watches it.

Mum watches it.

Noodle watches it.

"It's raining on the little boat," says Mo.
"But it's OK because it's going to take
away the sadness and I know it'll
be brighter soon."

The next morning, Mo is waiting in
the playground for Midge.

As soon as he appears, Mo races over.
"Hello, Midge. I've brought you a present."

Midge shakes his head because he
doesn't want presents. Mo reaches into
her school bag and brings out the little
homemade glitter jar.

Midge's eyes widen as Mo shakes it.

He watches the glitter fall
on the little boat.

"It's like a globe I have at home and
I wanted you to have one, too. It looks like
falling raindrops," whispers Mo, handing
Midge the jar, "and teardrops, too."

Midge is puzzled.

"Look," says Mo, pointing to the sunflower in the flower patch. "The flower has opened today." Mo tells Midge it came out after the rain fell. "Rain helped the plant and tears help us, too. That's because it's OK to cry when we're sad. *Everyone* feels sad sometimes." Mo smiles. "And do you know what happens after the rain?"

Midge shakes his head.

He doesn't know.

"The sun comes out," says Mo.

Midge looks down at the
globe in his hand. He gives it a shake.
It rains glitter on the little boat.

The words tumble out of his mouth.

"The sun is going to come out, one day?"
He feels a tiny tear run down his cheek but
quickly wipes it away with his sleeve.

"Yes," whispers Mo.

Midge shakes the globe again and watches
as the glitter falls and he smiles. It's the first
time he's smiled in his new school.

"You can shake it any time you feel sad,"
suggests Mo. "And the boat will take
away the sadness."

Midge feels the invisible rain cloud above him disappear. It's not raining any more. Not today. No more *drip-drip-drip.*

"Would you like to play football, Midge?" asks Mo, and Midge nods.

Mo lets Midge score a goal...

...and at lunchtime she offers him a
biscuit, which Midge accepts.

But then as soon as lunch is over, Mo
disappears and Midge feels the rain cloud come
back again and he goes and sits under the tree
in the playground by himself. *Drip-drip-drip.*

He feels a tear running down his cheek
as he shakes the globe over and over.

A few minutes later, Mo
comes running over, smiling.

"I had to go and get something."
She holds up the label from above
Midge's coat hook.

Mo has drawn
a beautiful big
sunflower and a
rain cloud beside
the sun she drew
earlier.

"Rain and tears –
both are important,"
says Mo proudly.
"Sun and happiness,
too."

She points to
the drawing and
underneath in
big rainbow letters
it says...

will you be my friend?

Mo smiles at Midge.

Mo smiles A LOT.

Midge looks up and sees the sun
coming out from behind a cloud.
*Maybe this new beginning isn't
going to be so bad after all, just
like Mum said*, thinks Midge.

Midge nods at Mo and
smiles through his tears.

"Yes, Mo," says Midge, sniffing.

"I'd like that very much."